Walt Disney's
Donald Duck's
Christmas Tree

A GOLDEN BOOK · NEW YORK
Western Publishing Company, Inc., Racine, Wisconsin 53404

It was the day before Christmas.

At Donald Duck's house, the cookies were all baked. The presents were all wrapped. It was time to get the Christmas tree.

Donald put on his coat and cap and mittens. He picked up his shiny ax.

"Come along, Pluto," he called. "We're going to the woods to find our Christmas tree." Pluto was visiting with Donald because Mickey was away for the holidays.

Pluto came on the run, and off they went into the snowy woods.

Now, deep in the woods in a sturdy fir tree lived two
merry chipmunks, Chip 'n' Dale. They were getting
ready for Christmas, too. They had found a tiny fir tree
standing in the snow near their home. They were
trimming it with berries and chains of dry grass when
Donald and Pluto came along.

The chipmunks heard Donald whistling in the woods. Then they saw Pluto prancing at his side. They scampered home to safety. At least, they thought they were safe.

But Donald took one look at their sturdy tree and said, "This is just the tree for us!"

Chop, chop, chop went Donald's shiny ax. Poor Chip 'n' Dale were too frightened to think.

"Come on, Pluto," called Donald when the tree was down. "Let's take our tree home."

So through the woods went Donald Duck, whistling as he tramped along, dragging the fir tree home.

And among the branches sat Chip 'n' Dale, having a very nice ride.

Donald set up the tree in his living room as soon as he got home.

"There," he said when he was through. "It's time to trim the tree." Donald brought out boxes of ornaments.

From their hiding place up in
the branches, Chip 'n' Dale looked
on. They watched Donald loop long
strings of colored lights over the
branches of the tree.

They watched him hang bright-colored balls of gold and red and blue. Pluto helped where he could.

"There!" said Donald as he hung the last ball. "Doesn't that look fine?"

And indeed it was a beautiful Christmas tree.
"Now I'll pile everybody's presents under the tree,"
said Donald. "Pluto, you stay here. I'll be right back."
"Bow-wow!" said Pluto as he sat down to admire the
Christmas tree.

As soon as Donald was out of sight, Chip 'n' Dale started to have fun.

They danced on the branches until the needles quivered.

They made faces at themselves in the shiny colored balls and laughed until their little sides shook.

"Grrr," growled Pluto disapprovingly.

But Chip 'n' Dale did not care. Chip just picked off two shiny balls and threw them at Pluto!

Pluto caught them in his paws.

"Grrr!" he growled crossly again.

Then Dale picked off another ball and threw it at Pluto, too!

Pluto jumped and barely caught it in his teeth. Just then, in walked Donald Duck.

"Pluto!" he cried. "Stop it!" He thought Pluto had been snatching balls from the tree.

Poor Pluto! There was not a sign of Chip 'n' Dale.

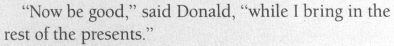

"Now be good," said Donald, "while I bring in the rest of the presents."

No sooner had Donald gone than Chip 'n' Dale appeared once more. Plunk! Chip put a cracked plastic ball over his head. Dale laughed and laughed.

But Pluto did not think it was funny at all. They were spoiling Donald's tree!

"Grrr!" he growled, getting ready to jump.

"Pluto!" cried Donald Duck from the doorway. "What's the matter with you? Do you want to ruin the tree?"

Of course, Chip 'n' Dale were safely out of sight. Poor Pluto could not explain.

"Now you'll just have to go outside and stay in the yard for the rest of Christmas Eve," said Donald sternly.

But just then, up in the treetop, Chip grew tired of wearing his round golden mask. He pulled off the ball and let it drop.

Crash! It bounced off the floor.

"What was that?" cried Donald.

"Bow-wow!" said Pluto, pointing to the tree.
Dale began to play with the colored lights, twisting them so they turned on and off.

"What's this?" cried Donald Duck.

"Bow-wow! Bow-wow!" said Pluto, pointing again. Donald peered among the branches until he spied Chip 'n' Dale.

"Well, well," he said, chuckling, as he lifted them down. "So you're the mischief-makers. And to think I blamed poor Pluto. I'm sorry, Pluto," said Donald.

Pluto marched over to the door and held it open. He
thought Chip 'n' Dale should go out in the snow.

"Oh, Pluto!" cried Donald. "It's Christmas Eve. We
must be kind to everyone, even pesky chipmunks. The
spirit of Christmas is love, you know."

So Pluto made friends with Chip 'n' Dale. They said they were sorry, in chipmunk talk.

And when Donald's nephews, Huey, Dewey, and Louie, came by to sing carols, eat cookies, and drink eggnog, they all agreed that this was by far their happiest Christmas Eve ever.